T0065520

KELLI CAMPBELL

Confronting
A
hero

authorHOUSE®

AuthorHouse™
1663 Liberty Drive
Bloomington, IN 47403
www.authorhouse.com
Phone: 833-262-8899

Published by AuthorHouse 01/28/2021

ISBN: 978-1-6655-1565-8 (sc)
ISBN: 978-1-6655-1566-5 (e)

Print information available on the last page.

Dedication

Huashi Vajhmood
Anne Wettschreck

Acknowledgments

I would like to thank my friends and family for letting me write this book and for supporting me so much love all of you.

Contents

Chapter 1

In The Night

IN THE MIDDLE OF A dark snowy forest. There lays an old rundown, falling apart school. In front of that school is a garden with a dirt road to get to the school. On that dirt road are two girl's walking to the school. One girl has medium brown curly hair with red highlights she has black jeans and a cat shirt on her name Lilly. Lilly's style was cute and simple. The other girl's name was Nikki and she was wearing ripped black jeans and a black crop top. She was also wearing black high heels. Nikki's hair was long, black with pink highlights. Nikki's style was bad girl the girl's were walking to school when it started to snow.

"The snow is pretty right Nikki?" Lilly asked

"Yea it is but don't you think your shoes are-" replied Nikki

"What about my shoes?" Lilly said cutting Nikki off

"Lilly your wearing sandals, and there's snow on the ground and it's snowing" Nikki said Laughing a little

"So your wearing ripped jeans and high heels" Lilly said raise an eyebrow

"Fine we both win" Nikki said

The girl's laughed and talked together as they walked to school. When they got into school a throwing knife went right by Nikki's head. Nikki turned around and saw Sol standing there. Sol was tall had Black hair he wore blue jeans that were ripped at the knees he also wore black boots with a white t-shirt gloves on his hands and lastly he wore a holder for his knife.

"What the heck Sol!" Nikki screamed

"What! I wasn't going to hit you" Sol replied

"Yea sure you weren't going to hit me" Nikki said as she pulled the throwing knife out of the wall

"I'll take that" Sol said holding out his hand Nikki took the knife and cut Sol's hand

"This is mine now" Nikki said putting the knife in her pocket

"Oh come on Nikki" Sol whined

"you're the one who threw it" Nikki snapped back

Just then Lilly grabbed Nikki's arm and started to shake her

"Look there's Luka" Lilly said looking at Luka

"oh my god you should go talk to him" Nikki said pulling her arm out of Lilly's grip

"What! Are you crazy?" Lilly screamed

"Hey Luka" Nikki said waving her hand

Luka was tall blonde and had a bicker style he was wearing ripped black jeans, a white tank top with a cross necklace and a leather jacket.

"Hey Nikki" Luka said

"Hey Luka are you free after school?" Nikki asked

"I think so why?" Luka asked

"Want to hang with us after school" Nikki said

"Sure why not see you guys later" Luka said walking away

Then the bell rang for class Nikki, Lilly and Sol walked to class together. Nikki and Lilly's first class was gym. Sol's first class was a cooking class. In gym Nikki and Lilly were practicing fighting.

"Hey Nikki where are we going after school?" Lilly asked as she dodge a punch

"I don't know probably Mr. cats café" Nikki replied as she did a backflip to avoid Lilly's attack

Then Nikki caught Lilly off guard and swung her leg under Lilly feet making her fall

"I won" Nikki said helping Lilly up

"You cheated" Lilly replied

"In a fight it doesn't matter" Nikki pointed out

"I guess your right" Lilly said

Then the bell rang. Lilly and Nikki walked to there next class which was history with Sol. Lilly walk in and was talking with Sol when Nikki walked in she was greeted by max. Max was tall had short brown hair always wore a suit a watch on his right wrist and he wore nice dress shoes.

"Hey beautiful" Max said with a wink

Nikki rolled her eyes this happened every day "Hey Max"

"How are you doing today?" Max asked

"I'm doing fine thanks for asking" Nikki replied

"Well I should get to my seat" Nikki added

Then the bell rang to start class. Class was going well until the teacher pair people up, and of course Nikki and Max were pair together. Nikki walked over to Max's desk and sat down next to him. She sighed and looked over at Max.

"Looks like were partners" Nikki said

"I guess we are kitten" Max said with a smile

"Kitten?" Nikki cringed at the pet name

"Do you not like it?" Max asked

"Not really" Nikki said

"Why not?" Max asked

"There's too many pet name just pick one" Nikki said

"I can do that" Max said

Class was good after that. After school Nikki, Lilly, Sol and Luka went to Mr. cats café. When they got in Lilly and Sol got a table as Nikki and Luks got the drink's.

"What are you going to get?" Nikki asked Luka

"I think I'm going to get a caramel latte you?" Luka asked

"Chai tea" Nikki said

Nikki and Luka were talking when they got there drink's. They got the drink's and went over to the table where Lilly and Sol were sitting.

"Hey guys thanks for the drinks" Lilly said

"No problem" Luka said

Luka and Lilly sat next to each other. Nikki and Sol sat next each other. They had fun talking, Laughing and just being teens. They spent two hours at the cafe they said goodbye to each other. Sol and Luka Went one way and Lilly and Nikki went the other way.

"That was nice" Nikki said

"What do you mean?" Lilly asked

"Don't you ever miss being a teenage?" Nikki asked

"We are teenagers Nikki" Lilly replied

"Were not normal we will never be normal!" Nikki yelled

"Wow Nikki clam down" Nikki said

"I'm sorry My wolf came out" Nikki said

"Umm Okay let's go home" Lilly said a little confusion

When they got home Nikki went up to her room and Lilly chilled in the living room. When Nikki was in her room her wolf came out and she trashed her room. At six Lilly knock on Nikki's door.

"Nikki?" Lilly asked

"Go away" Nikki snapped

"Nikki are you crying?" Lilly asked

"No" Nikki said

"Nikki open the damn door!" Lilly yelled

After a while Lilly heard a click and the door opened. When Lilly walked into Nikki room she was shocked. Nikki was on her bed crying there were papers everywhere, books all over her room was a mess.

"Nikki why are you crying?" Lilly asked

"I can't find my choker" Nikki whisper as a tear rolled down her cheek

"Nikki don't worry we'll find it"

Nikki just nodded her head slowly then Nikki's phone rang it was Sol.

"Hey Sol what's up?" Lilly asked answering Nikki's phone

"Hey Lilly?" Sol said sounding confused

"Yea Nikki Busy right now" Lilly replied

"Oh okay I'll call back later" Sol said hanging up

"Okay bye Sol" Lilly said ending the call

After the phone call Nikki and Lilly clean up Nikki's room and they found her choker. The next day after school Nikki and her friends were hanging out in the garden of the school. When a braided bracelet hit Luka in the head.

"Ow!" Luka said

"What even hit you?" Sol asked

"Common sense" Nikki said laughing

"Ha-ha very funny" Luka said rolling his eyes

Nikki just smirk while she leaned against a tree. "Omg I'm so sorry" A girl said. She had long hair that kinda went over her blue eyes on the left side. Her blue jeans were ripped at the bottom with a white t-shirt with a red and white flannel tied around her waist.

"Omg I'm really sorry" The girl said

"It's fine what's your name?" Luka asked

"Frankie" she replied

"Oh cool you want to chill with us?" Lilly asked

"No sorry I would love to but my mom wants me home to help in the barn and with the horse's" Frankie replied

"No problem also here your bracelet back" Luka said handing Frankie back her bracelet

"Thanks well see you guys later" She said walking away

"I like her" Lilly said

The friends stayed there till it was almost night. They all got up and went home. When Nikki and Lilly got home they both went up to there rooms.

"Don't trash hour room this time" Lilly joked

"I'll try" Nikki replied

When the girls got in there rooms they change into comfy clothes and turned on there TV's. It was about ten o'clock when Nikki turned on the news.

"There's been a shooting downtown one killed" the news reporter said

"Omg that's bad we can't have that happening" Nikki said

"Well let's go shadow"

With that Nikki jumped out her window into the darkness.

Chapter 2

The Fight

A<small>S</small> N<small>IKKI</small> <small>JUMPED</small> <small>OUT</small> <small>OF</small> her window she transformed into her wolf. "Shadow claws out!" Nikki yelled

Sparkles surrounded Nikki as a mask covered her face. Her blue eyes turned into a mint color, she was wearing black boots, a black jumpsuit with a light blue crescent moon by her chest. As she jumped onto the rooftops of buildings. She meet up with Lilly and Sol who also turned. Lilly's green eyes turned white her face was also cover with a mask. She was wearing gray flat shoes and a gray jumpsuit. Sol's black eyes turned red, his face was cover by a mask. He was wearing a dark blue almost black jumpsuit with a holder to carry his gun.

"Hey sugar, Sup Luna" Shadow said

Lilly turned into a grey cat called Sugar and Sol turned into a fox demon called Luna.

"I'm Guessing you saw the news?" Sugar asked

"Yea" Shadow and Luna replied

They all stopped on a rooftop looking over a book store

"Why a bookstore?" Shadow asked

"Maybe he wanted a book" Sugar answer

"Well he won't get to read it" Shadow added looking at sugar

Suddenly a group of guys came out of an ally. One of the guys was carrying a duffel bag and then guys followed him, then he pulled out a gun and pointed it at the guys.

"Oh no well this just got bad" Sugar said

"Hey Luna?" Shadow asked

"Yea what's up" Luna replied looking up from cleaning his gun

"Think you can make the shot" Shadow said raising a brow

"Who do you think I am" Luna said as he threw his gun over his shoulder

"I think you're a idiot" a voice said

Shadow hear Luna cursed under his breathe when he heard the voice.

"Hi Cat" Shadow while sitting on the edge of the building

"How has he not shot anyone yet?" Sugar asked leaning on the same edge Shadow was sitting on looking at the people below them

"I was just going to go" Luna said glaring at cat

"Want me to come with you?" Cat said winking at Luna "Luna just go" Shadow said getting a little mad

Luna nodded and jumped away to get a better shot

"Cat you have an interesting choice of clothing on tonight" Shadow said looking at Cat

Cat had black laced high heel boots. A holder about half way up her leg with a shotgun in it. Black tights shorts a white tank top with a black hat that says B.A.D

Yea your point?" Cat asked

"Nothing you just look badass" Shadow said looking over the edge

"Has Luna still not shot him yet" Cat said rolling her eyes

"He has to find the perfect spot" Sugar said almost falling asleep

Then they all hear a gun shot. Cat walked over and looked over the edge.

"He missed" Cat said smiling

"No he didn't" Shadow challenge

The bullet that Luna shot went over the man's head. Hit a metal pipe and hit the man in the back of his head. The man fell to the ground and dropped the gun.

"Let's go Sugar" Shadow said while jumping over the edge of the building

"Uh Finally" Sugar said following Shadow

Sugar landed on the ground behind a guy and kicked him in the head. Shadow landed on a guy's back making him fall.

"That's one way to take them out" Sugar said as she punch a guy in the face

Shadow just smile as she jump spun and kick aa guy and sent him flying almost hitting Sugar.

"Sorry Sugar" Shadow said doing a backflip to avoid a guy's fists

"Yours good" Sugar replied

Shadow was then taken by Surprise when a guy came up behind her and, pointed at gun at her head. The guy started to back up with Shadow. Sugar was to busy fighting three guys. Then Luna joined Cat on the rooftop and saw Shadow in trouble. Cat pulled out her handgun and shot the guy's hand he drop the gun but keep his hold on Shadow.

"What the heck Cat" Luna asked

"What let her finish him off" Cat said

"How is she supposed to finish him when he still has a grip of her!" Luna said raising his gun and shooting him

The guy dropped Shadow looked up at Luna and gave him a nod. Luna just nodded back. After a couple of minutes Shadow and Sugar joined the group back of the rooftop.

"I'm going to go it's pretty late and I need a nap" Cat said

"Are you going to have a cat nap" Luna teased

Cat glared at Luna

"Come on guys let's go home I'm also tired" Sugar said

The group agreed and went home. In the morning Nikki and Lilly got ready and went to school. When they walked into school. The fire alarm went off.

"What the hell?" Sol yelled

"When did you get here?" Nikki asked

"I was right behind you" Sol replied

The group ran outside and saw something they thought they would never see. There school was on fire.

Chapter 3

A New Beginning

THE GROUP STOOD THERE ABSOLUTELY shocked at what they were looking at.

"What are we supposed to do now?" Sol asked

"I have no idea" Nikki said slowly

School was let out early because of the fire. Everyone went home expect the group there life was in that school. The group stayed there until dark. Then Frankie showed up at the school.

"What are you guys still doing here?" Frankie asked

"Being sad" Luka said

"Why?" Frankie asked

"It's gone get it threw your head" Frankie added as she walked away

"Don't talk about something you know nothing about" Nikki snapped

Everyone was shocked with Nikki's comeback

"What do you want me to say sorry your school burned down!" Frankie yelled

"You know nothing about that school, you know nothing about my life my friends life. You have no right to talk about our school" Nikki said

"Our life was in that school" Luka whisper

Everyone agreed Frankie had no idea that school was so important. That night the group of friends stayed in the forest and told stories about there school. They started a fire so they would stay warm. The next day Nikki woke up on a tree branch. She looked down and saw Lilly and Luka snuggled up together. Sol was above her in another tree branch. Everyone got up stretched and yawned.

"What are you doing up there Nikki?" Lilly asked rubbing her eyes

"I guess I wanted to sleep in a tree" Nikki replied

"Wait why is Sol in a tree branch too?" Luka asked

"Cause he's weird" Lilly said

"I'm not weird" Sol said sitting up

"Oh look the princess is up" Lilly said as her and Nikki laughed

"Very funny now who's hungry" he said climbing down the tree

"Let's go to Mr. cats café" Sol added

The group arrived at Mr. cats café. Lilly invited Frankie they all sat down. Boys on one side girls on the other

"This is so uneven" Sol said picking up a menu

"I can invite Abby" Nikki said smiling

"No, no I'm fine" Sol said glaring at Nikki, while everyone laughed

"Good morning everyone" Mr. Cat greeted

"Good morning Mr. Cat" Everyone greeted back

The group order and talked for a while. Feeling like real teenagers. Till Monday all the friends got a call from angle school saying that they will all be attending. Nikki called everyone to the park to talk about that call.

"I'm not going to another school" Lilly said sitting down next to Nikki

"What choice do we have?" Nikki asked

"It's our senior year we have too" Luka said

"Fine I will go but I won't like it" Lilly mumble

"I never said you had to love it" Luka said smiling

"We should go home and get ready for tomorrow" Sol suggests

The group said goodbye and went home to get ready. Nikki's alarm went off at six-forty five in the morning. Nikki got up and put on her school uniform. The school uniform was a dark navy blue dress with two white stripes on the bottom and writs. Knee high socks with three white stripes on the top, white shoes and a white uneven bow tie. Nikki and Lilly got ready for school they walked outside and Luka was there waiting for them.

"Luka what are you doing here" Lilly said

"And in a mini van" Nikki added

"I'm here to pick you up and don't hate on the van" Luka explain

Nikki just rolled her eyes. They got in the van where Sol, Abby, Luka and Frankie were all sitting waiting for them. Luka was driving Abby was in the passenger seat. Frankie was behind Luka and Sol was in the middle.

"Uh there only one seat left where is Nikki going to sit?" Lilly asked

"She can sit on my lap" Sol joked

"Good idea Abby got sit on Sol's lap" Nikki said

"Okay" Abby agreed

Abby got out of the car and reentered the car sitting on Sol's lap. Lilly got in and shut the side door. Nikki got in the passenger seat and closed the door. The group was off to a new school. Luka pulled into the school parking lot. The school was huge it was a all white brick building it was four story's tall and long.

"Oh my god how people go here?" Abby asked

"Like a million" Frankie replied

"One hundred and ninety five" Luka said

"Why do you know that?" Nikki asked

Luka just smiled as he put the van in park. The group got out of the car and started walking. Nikki and Sol were behind the rest of the group talking.

"I hate you right now" Sol replied

"You know you love me" Nikki joked

"Also what are you wearing Sol?" Nikki asked

Sol was wearing black dress shoes and, like the girl uniform it was a dark navy blue set. The pan5s and the top were the dame color the top had Five gold buttons.

"The school uniform" Sol replied

"Your also wearing a dress Nikki" Sol added

"Whatever don't get use to it" Nikki replied

"But now I get to see you five days a week in a dress" Sol said teasingly

"And I get to see you five days a week in that" Nikki said

"I don't like it either" Sol said nudging Nikki

Sol and Nikki joined Luka, Lilly, Abby and Frankie in the schools entered. There was white brick on the inside with marble floors.

"Holy crap" Abby said

"Did we just walk into Heaven" Frankie asked

"Are we sure were not dead?" Lilly asked

"I'm sure were not dead" Nikki answered looking at Lilly

"Are you sure?" Frankie asked

"Yes" Luka responded

"Hello there" A voice said

The group turned around and saw a women in black high heels, a black dress with a gray blazer. She had Long light brown hair with greens eyes. She looked in her mid 30's

"Hi" The group said

"My name is Claire and I'm the head mistress of the school"

"We didn't walk into heaven we walked into an anime" Nikki said looking at Frankie

"I still think we walked into heaven" Frankie replied

"Guys we walked into a school now behave" Luka said

"Whatever" Nikki said rolling her eyes

Then two people walked beside the head mistress one was a girl, she was kind of short had long black hair and brown eyes. She also wore the school uniform. The other person was a boy he had short brown blondish hair with brown eyes. He also wore the school uniform.

"Hello I'm Tammy" The girl said

"Hello I'm Cody" The boy said

"We are so glad to have you in our school, but our school Is not like your school so be nice and you'll be fine" Claire said

"She knows she's talking to me?" Nikki asked

"She'll fine out" Lilly replied

The women smiled and walked away. The group and the two people just stood there staring at each other.

"Me and Cody will show you around come on" Tammy said

Tammy showed the group around. They were all amazed at the sizes of it. The end of the day came and the group got into the van and went home. About a week later Nikki went out for a run. She was walking to cool off. When she looked over to the right and saw Max Nikki walked over to Max.

"Hi Max" Nikki said waving

"Hello Kitty" Max said

"Kitty?" Nikki asked

"Soft but fierce" Max said with a wink

"Oh god" Nikki said rolling her eyes

"How have you been you look good" Max said

Nikki was wearing a hoodie crop top with black leggings. White and black shoes. Max looked at his watch he said bye to Nikki then left in a hurry. Nikki looked at Max's back confused so she followed him. Nikki followed Max to a large warehouse she didn't see him it started to rain so she ran into the warehouse. It was cold and dark in the warehouse she saw something in the corner of her eye. The Shadow was short and kind of skinny. Nikki creped closer and saw Max At least she think's she did it was dark.

"What do you mean you can't find it!" Max shouted

"I put it in a box" The boy said

"And" Max pushed

"I lost the box" The boy said looking down

"Ollie you idiot I need that box" Max said

"I need to go" Nikki said

Chapter 4

Another Fight

NIKKI WAS BACKING UP WHEN she tripped on a wire on the floor. She fell back with an "Oof" her hand went up to her mouth but it was too late.

"What was that?" Max said

Max started looking around he was only two feet away from Nikki. She was behind some boxes then she had an idea Nikki put on her black choker.

"Shadow claws out" Nikki whisper

Sparklers surrounded Nikki and she transformed but this time her outfit was different instead of a black jumpsuit she had black high heel boots, black pants and a black crop top with a black mask. Shadow jumped up on a box then jumped to grab a pipe and crouched down she watched Max as best she could then lost him in the darkness she suddenly hear Max.

"Bear let's go"

There was a flash of light and Max transformed he had black boots, black pants and a white and a red coat that went down to the floor. He also had a mask his mask was black and red mixed together. Bear walked over and pushed a button that turned on the lights Shadow just watched him. Ollie had also turned he had a jumpsuit that was half grey and half blue. Ollie's name had also changed now his name was Comet.

"Comet bring that box over here" Bear said

Comet set a box in front of Bear. Shadow leaned forward and casted a shadow on the box.

"What the" Bear said

Bear looked up and saw nothing before Bear looked up Shadow jumped a grabbed a cord that was hanging down from the ceiling. Shadow climbed down from the cord she crept around and hid behind some boxes. "*I have to stop this but how*" Shadow thought. Then she got an idea

"Hello" A voice said

"Hey Blaze it's Shadow"

"Hey Shadow what's up why are you so quiet?" Blaze asked

"Umm I'm in a bit of a pickle" Shadow replied

"Okay I'm on my way" Blaze said ending the phone call

Luka put on his blue and white ankle bracelet

"Blaze fire up!" Luka said

Blaze had a black costumes with red lines and a black mask. Along with Blaze he had a katana. Blaze showed up at the warehouse and found Shadow.

"Hey Shadow"

"Hey Blaze"

"Uh Blaze?" Shadow asked

"Yea Shadow" Blaze replied

"Why do you have a katana?" Shadow asked

"Found it in my garage" Blaze replied

"Why do you have a katana in your garage?" Shadow asked

"Not important why did you need my help?" Blaze asked

"Cause It's two against one" Shadow said

"Wait so you wanted a fair fight" Blaze said

"Yea kind of" Shadow said

"What do you want me to do?" Blaze asked

"I want you to go to the right up to the pipes crawl across and drop behind those boxes" Shadow explained

"Okay got it" Blaze said nodding

Blaze did what Shadow told him to do. While he was doing that someone drop behind Shadow. She kicked one in the stomach and slapped the other one.

"Ow" one of them said

"You slapped me" the other one said

Shadow knew one of the voices

"Luna?" Shadow asked

"Hey Shadow" Luna said getting up

"Did I slap you that hard?" Shadow asked

"Kind of you slapped me and I tripped" Luna said

"I'm Still down here" The other voice said

"Oops Yea sorry about that" Shadow said helping the person

"I'm Midnight"

"Well Midnight It's nice to meet you"

Midnight was wearing red heels, black shorts a camo crop top, a black mask and red gloves. Luna was wearing black boots, black chain leggings a gray belt a Gray T-shirt and a black mask. Midnight went over to help Blaze. Shadow and Luna stayed. Blaze looked at Shadow. Shadow nodded then they attacked. Blaze and Midnight attacked Comet and Shadow and Luna attacked Bear. Shadow punched Bear, Bear stumble backward he picked up a pipe and charged at Luna. Luna jumped back did a backflip and landed on his hands and knees. He was fine Luna ran back to the boxes and grabbed his gun and place it on top. Bear kicked Shadow then swiped his leg and made her fall then he got on top of her and pinned down her wrist. Comet had already tied up Blaze and Midnight.

"Your going to regret hitting me" Bear said

"As if" Shadow said

"Comet get the gun" Bear said

"Yes sir" Comet said bringing over a gun

Comet pointed a gun at Shadow. Shadow's eyes widened as she struggled even more. Luna was lining up a shot with a metal pipe. While this was happening Midnight was trying to get her hands free. Luna pulled the trigger and the bullet went flying threw the air. It hit the pipe with a big clack. After it hit the pipe Luna jumped over the boxes and tackled Comet. Comet fell to the ground along with the gun. Luna ran towards the gun but Comet got to it first and started shooting Luna Jumped kicked Comet and Comet went flying backwards. Luna ran over and untied Blaze and Midnight. Midnight ran over to Shadow and tackled Bear. Shadow got up and ran over to Luna and Blaze.

"Where'd they go they were just here?" Shadow asked

"They have to be here let's look around" Blaze Suggested

"Okay let's do that" Shadow agreed

The group looked around the warehouse for two hours they found nothing so they left. When Shadow got home she went to bed, but she couldn't sleep she came so close to being shot. She finally went to bed at one in the morning. Nikki got up and got ready for school, she met Luka and the group outside.

"Hey guys" Nikki said while getting in the van

"Hey" The group said

"Wow Luka, Sol you guys look like shit what happened?" Nikki asked Luka had a small cut on his cheek and rope burns on his hand. Sol had a big gash on his arm and a black eye.

"Uh fist fight" Luka said

"I fell" Sol said

"Shouldn't it be the other way" Lilly said

"No" Sol said

"How did you get a black eye falling?" Abby asked

"Fell into a dumpster" Sol answers

"Can we go to school guys" Luka said

The group arrived at school and meet up with Tammy and Cody.

"Wow Sol, Luka you guys look rough" Tammy said

"Yea Luka got into a fist fight and Sol fell" Abby said

"shouldn't it be" Tammy was cut of by Nikki

"We already had that conversation" Nikki said

"Oh well class is about to start then" Tammy said

The group thought it was a normal day. It was lunch time and Nikki and Lilly were walking back to their friends.

"Oh no this is not happening" Lilly said

"What?" Nikki asked

"How about a girl trying to get your boy" Lilly replied

"Me and Cody aren't together" Nikki said

"Whatever I'm stopping this right now" Lilly said walking towards the guys

There were two girl's one's name was Crystal she was blonde, tall and really pretty. The other one was named Summer she had brown hair, short and pretty. Crystal was all over Luka and Summer was all over Cody. Lilly walked over and grabbed Crystal by the hair and punched her. Nikki came over and tripped Summer. Crystal got up and started to throw punches at Lilly. Lilly dodged every punch. Summer got up and attacked Nikki. Nikki just flipped her over and she landed on the ground. Lilly jumped kicked Crystal. Both the girls gave up and walked away.

"Luka are you okay?" Lilly asked
"Why did you do that!" Luka snapped as he walked away
"Luka" Lilly asked
"Cody?" Nikki asked
"Don't talk to me!" Cody snapped as he walked away

18

Chapter 5

The Mistake

———◆———

"C ODY WAIT" NIKKI SAID RUNNING after him
"What do you want?" Cody asked
"I'm sorry" Nikki said
"Well in that case your to late" Cody said turning around
"What do I have to say what should I do!?" Nikki screamed tears welding up in her eyes
Nikki couldn't hold it in any longer. She turned around ran away.
"Uh Nikki!" Cody said
"Wow you're an idiot" Lilly said leaning against the lockers
"So are you" Cody said raising a brow
"Yea but we made up" Luka said walking beside Lilly
"I feel like I made the worst mistake in my life"
"How about instead of feeling sorry for yourself you could go talk to her" Lilly said
"Will she even talk to me?" Cody asked
"For as long as I've know Nikki she'll give anyone a second chance" Luka said
"Okay I'll go" Cody said
Cody walked around the whole school he couldn't find Nikki. He went to the one place he always use to go to the roof.
"I though I'd find you up here" Cody said
"What made you think that?" Nikki asked
"Cause I use to come up here" Cody said looking out to the parking lot

Cody sighed "Nikki look I'm really sorry I didn't mean to snap I guess I just got mad in the moment and I took it out on you"

"Thanks Cody" Nikki said turning around

Then Cody sat down next to Nikki and he leaned in then they heard footsteps

"Guys!" Lilly said racing up the steps

"Um I'm I interrupting anything?" Lilly asked

"No!" Cody and Nikki yelled

Lilly just laughed

"Anyway guys Frankie didn't come to school today" Lilly said worrying

Cody and Nikki looked at each other and raised a brow.

"Frankie never miss school" Lilly said

"Lilly maybe Frankie's just sick" Nikki said

"Nope she's been kidnaped" Lilly said with a nod

"Where did you come up with that idea?" Cody asked

"I just have a feeling" Lilly said

"Okay well that's the bell I'm going to head back to class" Nikki said leaving

"Wait for us" Cody said

Meanwhile in another warehouse Bear had Midnight and he had big plans for her.

"How many warehouse's do you have like twelve?" Midnight asked while in a jail cell

"Oh so close I have ten" Bear said

"Wow so impressed" Midnight said

"Why thank-Hey!" Bear said

Midnight just laughed

"Ha Soon I'll get the last laugh" Bear said getting a control

"What's that supposed to mean?" Midnight asked

"You'll see" Bear said

Bear smiled and pushed the first button on the control. The jail had holes so Midnight could breathe. The air was stale cause it was a warehouse. This green gas started to come out and Midnight started to cough. Midnight's knee's gave out and she fell still coughing. She felt weak and sick.

"This gas will remove all of your powers and animalsness inside you. I will bottled it up and drink it then I will be the most powerful evil villain ever" Bear explained

"Animalness Isn't a word" Midnight said in between coughs

"What! Of course it's a word" Bear said

"And why is it a word?" Midnight asked

"Cause I said it is that's why" Bear said

"Okay then" Midnight said

"Wait is it really not a word?" Bear asked

"I don't know man maybe it is maybe it isn't" Midnight replied

"Ugh" Midnight groaned as she felt even weaker

"I'll leave you to your pain" Bear said as he walked away laughing

Midnight was so weak that she was slipping in and out of conscience but she was awake enough to hear Bear and Comet talking

"Now what boss?" Comet asked

"We wait and we get the other's" Bear replied

That was the last thing Midnight heard then everything went black. That night Shadow sat on top of a building she sat with one leg over the edge and the other on the building. Then she heard Sugar behind her. Sugar's outfit changed too she was wearing gray high heel boots, black pants a gray belt a black tank top, some black gloves and a black mask. Behind Sugar was Cat she was wearing black boots a gun holder on her left leg. Black jean shorts a black tank top. Her black hair was braided also she had a belt with ammo in it with a black mask. Behind Cat was Luna and Blaze

"When I said let's meet up I didn't think you'd all show up at the same time" Shadow said

"Guess we all didn't want to be late" Sugar said

"Actually I don't care if I'm late" Cat said

"Me too" Luna agreed

"Umm Luna?" Sugar asked

"Yes" Luna replied

"Where's your gun?" Sugar asked sitting down next to Shadow

"It's on my back why? I'm I going to use it?" Luna asked

"No you won't" Shadow said

"Why not?" Cat asked

"No" Shadow said

"Whatever" Cat said rolling her eyes

"Um Shadow?" Sugar asked

"Yea Sugar" Shadow replied

"Can I asked you a question?" Sugar asked

"What is this 20 questions" Cat said

"Shut up Cat! What is your question?" Shadow asked

"So I was out last night" Sugar got cut off

"Looking for a man" Luna said

""We all are" Shadow said

"Ahem anyway I met two people and kind of invited them to chill with us" Sugar explained

"Okay what are there names?" Shadow asked

"Star and Lumimous" Sugar said

Cat who was talking to Blaze whipped her head around.

"Say that last name again" Cat said

"Lumimous" Sugar said again

The group talked for a while until Star and Lumimous arrived. They introduced themselves.

"Hi I'm Star" He said

"Hello I'm Lumimous" She said

Star was wearing an all black costume with gold lining and a star symbol on his chest. Lumimous was wearing black heels a black skirt a red no sleeve shirt and a black mask. The group sat and talked all night getting to know each other and catching up. The group met up at 9 at night now it was about 10. Shadow and sugar were sitting on the edge of a building and the rest of the group was sitting on the floor.

"Okay so I think we've all noticed that were missing a person" Shadow said

"We are?" Cat asked

"Yes Midnight right" Sugar replied

"Yes" Shadow replied

Shadow looked at Luna and nodded

"I know that look Shadow you have a plan" Luna said

"Your right I do" Shadow replied

"Okay well let's go save her" Cat said

"No" Shadow said
"What! Why?" Cat and Luna asked
"Because Bear will be expecting us" Shadow replied
"Okay well who do we send then?" Lilly asked
"Star and Lumimous"

Chapter 6

Rescue Mission

"Star and Lumimous" Shadow said

"What!" Star and Lumimous shouted

"Why us?" They asked

"Cause Bear won't be expecting you" Shadow explained

"You just met us" Star said

"And you trust us?" Lumimous aksed

"I Do" Shadow said

"You trust them not marrying them" Luna said while walking by

"I'm going to hurt you" Shadow said

"No you won't" Luna said smiling

"Guys let's not start a fight" Sugar said

"Whatever" Shadow and Luna both said at the same time

"Uh guys not to be rude but what's the plan?" Lumimous asked

"You two are going to sneak in find Midnight break her out and get out" Shadow explained

"Easier said than done" Blaze final spoke up

"And where were you this whole time?" Cat asked

"Thinking" Blaze said

"About?" Cat asked

"None of your business" Blaze replied with a smile

"Guys can we focus on the mission?" Shadow asked

"Fine" Cat grumbled

"Cool! Do you two know how to fight?" Shadow asked

"Umm No nothing" Lumimous replied

"I know a little" Star replied

Shadow sighed and then came up with a plan. Shadow and Blaze took Star and Sugar Luna and Cat took Lumimous. They split up and went to the other side of town. Shadow and Blaze stood on one side together and Star was on the other.

"Come at us" Shadow ordered

"Um I don't really feel comfortable doing that" Star said

"That wasn't a question that was an order" Shadow said

"Okay wait why?" Star asked

"We want to see what you can do" Shadow said

"How you fight" Blaze added

"Okay" Star said

Star started running at Blaze. Blaze jumped did a front flip and landed. Shadow caught Stars arm and flipped him. He landed on his back with an "Oof"

"Ow" Star said laying on his back

"When you said you know a little you really meant a little" Shadow said

"Yea" Star said

"Come on" Shadow said helping Star up

They trained again and again till Star couldn't get up. On the other side of town was Luna, Cat and Lumimous.

"Were going to test your speed" Luna said

"And how are you going to do that?" Cat asked

"With my gun" Luna replied

"Is that safe?" Lumimous asked

"Probably not" Luna replied

"Okay get running" Cat said

Lumimous started running and Luna started shooting and Lumimous ran faster. But she tripped and caught herself with a front flip. Then Cat got in the way and she slid under cat and tripped her and kept running after about 2 minutes of training Luna got a call.

"Hello?" Luna asked

"Luna we can hear your gun all the way across town!" Shadow yelled

"Oh you can" Luna said

"Yes what are you doing!?" Shadow asked

"Training" Luna replied

"Put the gun away now or I'll be coming over" Shadow said

"Okay" Luna said

The two groups practiced and trained till two in the morning. The group decided to call it's quite. Shadow returned home and turned back into Nikki. Nikki got ready for bed and went to sleep and so did the rest of the group. Meanwhile at the warehouse midnight had woken up and looked around. She was still in the same place she looked over and saw a bottle with a bluish clear liquid in it. It was halfway full Midnight knew what it was. It was her powers Midnight couldn't move or speak. She could barely hear as well she didn't know how long she had been in here and midnight was fighting.

"Boss I thought it would take a couple hours for her powers to drain" Comet said

"Nope it takes two weeks" Bear said

"Oh so she has one week to go?" Comet asked

"Yes so she has been here a week. One or more week and I'll have all her powers" Bear replied

Nikki woke up the next day at noon luckily it was a weekend so she didn't have to worry about school. It was late fall so when Nikki got up she put on some skinny jeans and a black long-sleeve t-shirt. Since it was noon Nikki did things around the house. After she was done she had a cup of tea and a text from Lilly. Lilly ask to meet up for dinner with the group. After dinner the group went to bed at 10 at night on Sunday Nikki woke up at 10 in the morning. Nicki went on with her day at night she met up with the group and trained before everyone went home Shadow had something to say.

"Guys we have been trainings for quite a while now. I say we save Midnight on Wednesday" Shadow said

Everyone agreed to this at school things were little awkward Cody and Nikki still haven't made up. Monday and Tuesday were fine then Wednesday came after school at about half-past eight the group met on top of a building on the rooftop. Shadow went over the plan with everyone.

"Okay Lumimous you'll go in thru the roof and sneak down and Find Midnight. Star you'll go in thru the widow and buy Lumimous some time" Shadow explained

Lumimous and Star got to the building and put the plan into action. Star crack the window with a brick.

"Star don't break the window" Lumimous said

"Then how I'm I going to get in?" Star asked

"Fine an open one" Lumimous replied

Star climbed in through an open window and Lumimous climb down from the rooftop. They both saw Bear and Comet they looked at each other and nodded. Star followed Comet when suddenly Comet turn around and punched Star. Star stumbled backwards and hit the ground with an oof. Star ran towards Comet punched him twice and jump kick him. Comet flew backwards hit a metal pipe and knocked himself out cold. *That was easy* Star thought and went to help Lumimous. Lumimous was still watching Bear. She leaned over to hear what Bear was saying but fell over. Bear heard and looked at Lumimous and started walking toward her. Star ran towards Bear and tackled him to the ground.

"GO!" Star shouted

Lumimous nodded and ran to find Midnight. Lumimous walked around the warehouse she came across a jail cell. She looked inside and saw Midnight laying on the ground. In the distance she heard fighting so she had to hurry. She saw the controller on the wall so she grabbed it and pushed the stop button. The green gas stopped and the jail cell opened it. Lumimous ran in and grabbed Midnight and the bottle that had her powers in it. Lumimous threw midnight on her back and walked towards the exit. As she was walking out she saw that Star was getting beaten up bad. Lumimous walked outside handed Midnight off to Shadow and ran back inside. Star had just gotten thrown against a metal pipe. Bear had a thick stick of wood. He was about to hit Star but Lumimous jumped in front and kicked the wood away and kicked Bear in the face grabbed his wrist and flipped him over. Lumimous ran over to Star and helped him up. The two hero's walked out of the warehouse and met up with the rest of the group. The group agreed that Star would stay with Lumimous and Midnight would stay with Shadow and Sugar. Then the group headed off towards home.

Chapter 7

Nightmare And Dreams

T HE GROUP HEADED HOME AND went to bed the first one to sleep was
Frankie. Frankie's nightmare started with the group on a rooftop.
The rest of the group went to fight and Midnight and Sugar were left
on the rooftop. As a joke Sugar took off Midnights braided bracelet.
Midnight was yelling at Sugar to give it back. She saw her bracelet blink
and then she started to turn back. Her costume disappeared then her mask
disappeared Frankie stood there. Frankie shifted in her sleep then went
back to sleep. The next to fall asleep was Lilly. It was after a fight and the
group was heading home Blaze followed Sugar home Sugar was in front
of her home and she looks both ways then took off or purple bracelet. 10
seconds later she was Lilly Blaze just stood there in awe. Lilly bolt it up
in her bed *"Oh what a horrible Nightmare"* She said. The third one to fall
asleep was Luka his started with training he was training with Shadow
and the rest of the group. Shadow and Blaze we're fighting with swords
Shadow jumped forward and ripped Blazers costume. *"Omg I'm so sorry"*
Shadow said *"It's fine"* Blaze replied. He refused to get it fixed and kept
training. After 10 minutes Blaze costume disappeared and then his mask
and Luka was standing there. The group was shocked. Luka eyes shot open
and put a hand over his eyes. *"Just a Nightmare"* Luka said. The fourth
to sleep was Tammy her and Cody were talking and then Cody notices a
small cut on her cheek and a burn on her arm. *"What happed?"* He asked
"Nothing" Tammy replied *"You were fighting weren't you"* Cody asked *"I
don't know what your talking about"* Tammy said *"Oh really Lumimous"*
Cody said *"How do you know?"* Tammy asked *"Come on everyone knows"*

Cody said. Tammy fell out of bed and woke up she got back in bed *"Only a Nightmare"* She said. The fifth to sleep was Cody. Tammy and Cody were talking Tammy was telling him about her friend who likes Star and Cody just snapped. *"I can't handle it anymore!"* Cody yelled *"Cody what is it?"* Tammy asked *"I'm Star"* Cody said. Cody woke up and rubbed his eyes *"Just a Nightmare"* He said. After Cody Abby went to sleep. Abby's alarm went off she shut it off and went to school. When she got to school people were giving her weird looks. She looked to her right and saw Sol. *"Sol?"* Abby asked *"Cat!"* Sol yelled. Abby look down and saw that she was dressed as Cat. Abby woke up " *Wow that was a weird nightmare"* she said. It was Sol's turn to sleep. His nightmare started with him and Cat fighting. Shadow showed up to watch the fight to make sire it was fair. They both drew there guns and started shooting Luna got hit in the arm. *"Luna!"* Shadow yelled as she ran over to him. She ripped his costume and his costume and mask disappeared. *"Sol!?"* Shadow asked Surprise. Sol sat up in his bed *"I hope this is just a Nightmare"* He said. Nikki went to bed next her nightmare started in a fight. Her and Bear we're fighting Bear was throwing punches and Shadow was dodging every one of them. The rest of the group was tied up she turned to look at the group and Bear punched her right in the face. Shadow fell to the ground. Bear walked up and ripped her mask off. Her Costume disappears *"Nikki"* The grouped yelled. Nikki bolted up from her bed. *"A nightmare just a nightmare"* she said. Max fell asleep fast. Max stood in a warehouse talking to his father. *"Dad I caught a hero"* Max Said *"Mm and where is this hero?"* His father asked

"Gone Father" Max replied. *"I'm really disappointed in you max"* Max's father said Max woke up. *Will I ever be good enough for you dad Max Thought.* Last to sleep was Ollie his was a happy dream. His dream was he got a couple boxes for Max. *"Ollie I'm so proud of you"* He said Ollie woke up and smiled *"What a good dream"* He said.

.

Chapter 8

The Truth Comes Out

T HE GROUP WENT TO SCHOOL the next morning and they all looked rough. The nightmares still haunted each one of them. It was lunch time and the group was talking they all said that they had nightmares. After school the group thought long and hard about their nightmares. How would they tell the group? Would they tell each other? How would they react? Everyone would react differently and that's what scared each one of them. Tammy couldn't sleep since her nightmare she had to come clean. She had to tell someone Tammy grabbed her phone and texted Cody *"Hey can we meet up?"* Tammy asked. As Tammy grabbed her gold chain necklace she heard her phone ding. It was Cody *"Sure"* was all he replied with. Cody grabbed his gold star ring and him and Tammy headed off to meet up. Star and Lumimous met on top of a office building.

"Hey Lu" Star said

"Lu?" Lumimous asked

"Short for Lumimous" Stat replied

"Oh that makes sense" Lu said

"What did you want to talk about?" Star asked

"Okay so" Lu started

Lu started to tell Star about her Nightmare and how she couldn't sleep and that she needed to tell someone. Star nodded and told Lu about his Nightmare and how he has been wanting to tell someone two. The two agreed that they would tell each other who they are.

"Okay on three" Lu said

"On three" Star said

"One" They said looking into each other eye's

"Two" there hands went up to there masks

"Three!" they both said taking off there mask's

Tammy and Cody stood there looking at each other

"Tammy!" Cody yelled

"Cody!" Tammy yelled

The two just stood there in shock they couldn't believe that they lied to each other. Tammy and Cody have been best friends since freshman year in high school. They talked for a while then went home Tammy and Cody felt much better after telling someone. Now they just had to tell the rest of the group. Lilly wanted to tell Luka because she loves him so she asked Luka to meet her at a coffee shop but she never showed. She got too scared and nervous she didn't answer his texts or calls and avoided him at school. Luka was really confused to why Lilly was acting this way so one night after school Blaze followed Sugar home. Sugar was out cause she needed some fresh air. She stopped in front of her house. She looked to the right and the left then took off her purple bracelet and Sugar turned back into Lilly. Blaze jumped off from the building behind Lilly and landed behind her. Lilly turned around and her eyes widened. It was just like her dream except Luka found her out but this guy looked familiar.

"Lilly" The man said

"How do you know my name?" Lilly asked

"Cause I know you" The man replied

"Do you" Lilly said

Blaze walked forward bended over and took off his ankle bracelet and Blaze turned into Luka.

"L-Luka!" Lilly asked now it was like her dream

"How could you?" Lilly asked

"I could asked you the same thing" Luka said

"I was scared I didn't know how you who react" Lilly said tears welled up in her eyes

"Is that why you didn't meet me?" Luka asked

Lilly started crying she was so ashamed that. He would think less of her.

"I'm so sorry Luka" Lilly said she couldn't see anything cause she was crying so much.

"Lilly I get where you're coming from" Luka said

Luka walked up to Lilly and hugged her. Lilly just cried none of them said a word they just stood there. After standing there Lilly stop crying. Luka kissed Lilly the kiss was only ten seconds long. After the kiss Lilly went inside and Luka turn back into Blaze and he went home. The school days were hard because some people new secrets and others didn't. The mornings were hard for Nikki cause she was looking after Frankie but she didn't know it was Frankie. She was still midnight Nikki gave midnight all her powers back. Now she was waiting for her to wake up. One weekend on a Saturday midnight's braided bracelet came off. Midnight turn back into Frankie and Nikki saw it happened. *No this can't be"* Nikki thought then Frankie woke up and saw a Nikki staring at her. Then she looked over and saw her braided bracelet then she understood what happened.

"Nikki I can explain" Frankie said

"No need" Nikki said

The next day Frankie and Nikki talked and work things out. Later that night Luna and Cat we're on a rooftop messing around and talking then Cat had a bad idea.

"Let's have a duel" Cat suggested

"Are you crazy?" Luna asked

"It's to early we have to wait" Luna asked

The two of them waited and waited then it was late enough and they started their duel. Cat drew her gun and loaded it Luna drew his gun and loaded it as well. Then they started shooting they were having fun until Cat got shot in the arm and Luna got shot in the leg. Cat ripped the end of her shirt she dug out the bullet then tied upper arm with the part of her shirt that she ripped. She went over and helps Luna with his leg. Then a strong gust of wind came and blew off Luna's and cat's masks. They sat there staring at one another.

"Abby!" Sol shouted

"Sol" Abby said

"You shot me" Sol said

"No you shot me" Abby said

"We shot each other" Sol said

Abby and Sol sat and talked for a while. One day after school Cody went to Nikki's house to see if they could talk. When he walked into

Nikki's bedrooms he saw Shadow. Shadow looked at Cody and took off her Choker and Shadow turned into Nikki.

"Nikki" Cody said

"Hi Cody" Nikki said

Cody and Nikki talked for a couple hours the next day at 10 o'clock. Shadow call a meaning on top of a building throughout good night the group slowly came together finally the whole group was there.

"I've called you here today because the truth needs to come out. We will all take off our mask's and accept each other as is" Shadow said

The group stood in a circle and all their hands went up to their masks and they all took them off.

Chapter 9

What Do We Do Now

THEY ALL TOOK THEIR MASKS off and looked around the circle and saw all there friends. Some of them knew ahead of time and others it was a complete shock. The group took turns telling the group about their nightmares that they had and how they kind of came true.

"Wait" Luka said

"What!" Everyone said

"What do we do now?" Luka asked

"We have to split up" Abby said

"What!" The group said

"Abby's right" Nikki said

"Wait are we deciding to break up our friendship" Lilly said

"I think we are" Sol added

"This is so sad" Lilly said

"Group hug" Nikki said

The group huddle together and hugged. They have been friends for as long as they can remember I've been through the best and the worst. Fights there have been plenty of those but they made up fast Cody and Tammy still they're unsure of what to do.

"Hey get in here guys" Shadow said

"Us?" They both asked

"Yea Your our friends too" Lilly said

Tammy and Cody join the hug the group then spent the rest of the night telling stories about the good old days and funny moments.

"And then….He fell into the pond" Lilly said as the group laughed except Luka

"Ha vey funny" Luka said

"They thought it was" Lilly replied

Luka just glared at her Lilly smiled the group went home and to bed. The next day Lilly and Luka walked over to wear Nikki, Sol and Abby were they were holding hands.

"You look happy" Nikki said

"I am" Lilly replied

"That's a first" Sol said

"Be nice you two" Abby said

"Oh your one to talk" Sol snapped back

"Uh back to Lilly and Luka please" Nikki said

"Sure" Abby said

"Whatever" Sol said

"Anyway we have something we want to tell you guys" Luka said

"Well then tell us" Abby said

"They were until you interrupted them" Nikki snapped back

"Well me and Luka are together" Lilly announced

"Girl finally" Nikki said

Nikki walked over to Lilly and gave her a hug and Luka walked over to Sol they bro hugged. They all sit around and talk till the bell ring for class they all grown they hated their classes here.

"I hate the class's here" Nikki said

"Yea you can't even sneak a throwing star in" Sol complained

The group left and went to class Sol went to cooking Luka went to gym Abby went to Mass and Nikki and Lilly went to history. The group knew that they had to split up soon but they were going to drag it out as long as they could. It lasted two months one day after school Nikki went to take a shower she went to her room and put on a pair of skinny jeans and a plain black V-neck t-shirt. She went to find her choker but she couldn't find it. She called Lilly and told her she said that she went to the kitchen to get some pop and when she came back purple bracelet was gone. Lilly came over to Nikki's house to talk. They were sitting on Nikki's bed talking for a while when Lilly brought up a good point.

"It's not like it just disappeared" Lilly said

Nikki gasp "Yes it did"

Nikki jumped off the bed and ran over to her desk and grabbed a piece of paper Lilly raised a brow.

"What is that?" Lilly asked

"The contract" Nikki said

Lilly formed a o with her mouth and nodded she got one too. Nikki held it close to her chest not wanting to look at it. She took a few deep breathes and was scared.

"God damn just look at it" Lilly said

"Okay okay gosh" Nikki said

Nikki unfolded the papers and reread the contracted that came with her piece of jewelry. The piece of papers said. " Dear Nikki you have been picked to be the wolf. You are like a wolf petty but mean that's just who I'm looking for

There are just a few rules you have to follow. one- You must only got out at night. Two- When in your wolf form your name is Shadow. Three- To turn into Shadow say "Claws out" Four- Don't and I repeat don't tell people who you are. Nikki and Shadow must not be connected okay well have fun."

That was the end of the note. Don't know who wrote it or why. The group has to be careful but they where about to find out. The next morning Nikki jewelry was on her night stand with a note a new note.

"I'm giving you one more chance don't mess up"

So rude Nikki thought Nikki put on some jeans and a white t-shirt. Then she went to go see the group

Turns out they all got that new note. So they went to mr. cats café to talk about it.

"What dose he mean he's giving up another chance!" Abby shouted as she slammed her hands down on the table.

"Abby calm down" Nikki said

"Nikki I'm with Abby on this one" Lilly said

"What why?" Luka asked

"Because what did we do wrong" Sol added

"We violated the contract" Nikki said

"What contract?" Abby asked

"The contract that said were heroes" Nikki replied

"I never agreed to that contract" Abby said

"Yes we all did" Luka said realizing what they agreed too.

"What do you mean Luka?" Lilly asked

"When we put on our piece of jewelry that was us agreeing to the contract" Luka explain

"Oh no we do have to spit up" Lilly said

Luka grabbed Lilly's hands telling her it's okay. Nikki slammed her hands down on the table and stood up

"That's it I'm finding out the truth the real truth" Nikki said

Chapter 10

The Truth Part 2

NIKKI WENT HOME AND LOOKED at the note. Then she called Frankie. Frankie's dad was a detective.

"Hello?" Frankie asked

"Hey Frankie it's Nikki" Nikki said

"Oh hey Nikki what can I do for you?" Frankie asked

"Your dad is still a detective right?" Nikki asked

"Yea Why?" Frankie asked

"I need something testes for fingerprints" Nikki replied

"Oh okay I can meet you in an hour" Frankie said

"Thanks I'll see you in an hour" Nikki said

Nikki grabbed both the notes and her piece of jewelry. She meet Frankie in a park Nikki walked up to Frankie.

"You ready?" Frankie asked

"Yes" Nikki replied

They got into a car and drove to Frankie's dad's work. The two girls got walked into the building and got a lot of weird looks. They finally found Frankie's dad.

"Hi daddy" Frankie said

"Oh hello sweetheart what can I do for you?" He asked

"I need fingerprints ran on these" Nikki said

"Oh Frankie can do that" He said

"You can?" Nikki asked

"Yea let's go" Frankie said

Frankie lead Nikki down the hallway and then down another hallway.

They entered a room and Frankie logged in. she took the papers from Nikki. It took an hour but she got some fingerprints. What Nikki heard next made her scared.

"Okay I got your fingerprints and someone named Matt" Frankie said

"wait did you say Matt?" Nikki asked

"yeah why?" Frankie asked

"Matts my brother" Nikki said

"your brother is behind this!" Frankie shouted

"I don't know" Nikki replied

"Well can't you talk with him tonight?" Frankie asked

"NO" Nikki snapped

"sorry it's just me and my brother don't get along very well" Nikki said

"Can I ask why?" Frankie asked

"He left us" Nikki said

"What!" Frankie said

"He left us to be a doctor" Nikki said

"Actually he's a lawyer" Frankie said typing on her computer.

"What?!" Nikki said surprised as she walked over to the computer

"Yup and he works at City Hall" Frankie said

"What time does he start?" Nikki asked

"uh eight but if you go now you can catch him right after his lunch break" Frankie explained

"You got a driver for me?" Nikki asked

"Better I got a car" Frankie asked

Nikki got into the black car and Frankie reminded her that she needed it back so Nikki invited her along. The ride was nice for Nikki it was scary for Frankie.

"how do you learn how to drive?" Frankie asked

"Video games" Nikki replied looking at Frankie then back at the road

"Just don't crash the car" Frankie said

"I've only crashed 2 times in the game then again I only play the game two times" Nikki said

"Oh god" Frankie said praying

Nikki parked the car and got out Frankie got in the driver's seat and said good luck and drove off. Nikki put on her choker and climbed the stone stairs to City Hall. Nikki enter City Hall and was shocked it was beautiful there was different colored stone everywhere the ground was a beautiful caramel color and the walls were white and black. Nikki walked over to a desk we're lady in her mid-30s sat at. She had curly red hair and was typing on her keyboard like crazy Nikki just stood there then coughed.

"What do you want?" The lady asked

Wow she so rude Nikko thought but said " Hi I'm looking for someone named Matt"

The lady stop typing and looked at Nikki "hun I going to need a last name we have ten people here named Matt"

Nikki sigh and said "Matt Star"

"Matt star" The lady said

"he's still on his lunch break you can wait over there" she said and pointed to a wall

Nikki just nodded and went over and leaned against the wall. Just us Nicky leaned against the wall her brother entered City Hall. Nikki's brother didn't look anything like her he had short brown hair clean shaven and green eyes. He had a suit on he entered City Hall with a woman she was shorter than Nikki's brother. She had blond hair with red highlights he kissed her goodbye and she left Nikki walked over to him and she was pissed.

"so you left your family to start a new one" Nikki snapped

"Nikki!" Matt said shocked

"What are you doing here?" Matt asked

"Just thought I'd visit my brother" Nikki said sarcastically

"BS" Matt said

"Why did you lie to us?" Nikki asked

"I was trying to protect you" Matt said

"From what?" Nikki asked

"From what?" Nikki asked again

"From ME!" Matt shouted

Nikki flinched at her brother's tone he's never yelled before. Matt saw Nikki flinch at his tone Matt's facial expressions softened. Nikki's eyes were wide and her face told you she was scared.

"I'm going to ask you one more time what do you want?" Matt asked

"What is this?" Nikki asked holding out the notes

Matt walked over and took the notes from Nikki he unfolded the notes and read them. He shook his head as he handed them back to Nikki.

"Sorry I don't know anything about it" Matt said

"Your fingerprints were on it" Nikki said

"Sorry I don't know I wish I could help you" Matt said

He turned around and started to walk away. Nikki was getting mad. Her heart on her choker started to glow.

"You don't get to walk away from this conversation!" Nikki shouted

"Oh look I'm going" Matt said

"Why do you always leave me" Nikki said

Matt stopped in his footsteps he turned around and walked right back over to Nikki.

"You know nothing about why I left" He said

"I wish I did I needed you" Nikki whispered the last part

"I'm sorry Nikki I love you" Matt said

"I love you too" Nikki said

They hugged and Matt started to walk away but before he left he said.

"Oh Nikki be careful of the Secret Soul Keeper" Matt said

"Matt! Matt!" Nikki keep shouting but he kept walking away.

Nikki sigh and walked outside it was raining. She was so mad that her brother was starting a new family. That he knows something and he not telling her. Her heart on her choker glowed even more white. That it actually turned her into a actual wolf. Her wolf was all black.

What the Nikki thought. She walked around as a wolf she thought and thought then realized this was what the note was talking about. This was there second chance. If they found out then they would have to break up there friendship. They can stay together. *I have to tell them* Nikki thought but first she had to change back. How Nikki turned back she took off her choker. She went back to her house. The next day Nikki called her friends and they agreed to meet her. They all meet up at Nikki's house. Nikki told them they were going for a walk. The group was walking for a while and found themselves at there old school. The group just stood there staring at what was left.

"This is why you came to our school" Tammy said

Everyone just nodded Nikki sigh and said " Guys I know what the second chance is"

"Well what is it?" Lilly asked

"I can't tell you" Nikki replied

"I can tell you that you have to get really mad about someone or something you really care about" Nikki said

Throughout the week the group one by one found out

Lilly is a grey cat, Sol is a fox with a red tail. Luka is a cheetah, Cody is a fennec fox. Tammy is a unicorn and Frankie is a black bear and Abby is an Owl at night and a hawk by day. The group was all freaked out but. Understood that they couldn't tell. They weren't going to fail this time. It was nearing senior year and the girl's were talking about prom. Lilly was hoping Luka was going to take her. It was about two weeks until prom and Luka asked Lilly. Of course Lilly said yes. About two days later Cody asked Nikki and Nikki said yes. At the end of the week Sol asked Abby and Abby said yes. All girls got ready. The night of prom finally came. All the guy's were wearing all black suits and there tie's matched the girls dresses. Luka tie was blue so Lilly's dress was blue. Cody's tie was red so Nikki's dress was red. Sol's tie was white so Abby's dress what white. They all got into a limo and went to prom the group had a great time. Tammy and Frankie found two guys to go to prom with sadly the great time had to come to an end. Nikki and Cody made up and got together Lilly and Luka got more close with each other and Sol and Abby got together. The group dropped Nikki off at home she got home showered and got into her PJ's then she found a note on her pillow.

"Hope you had fun but your not who you think you are from Matt A.K.A The Secret Soul Keeper (P.S It's time to confronting a hero)"

About The Author

I'm a young creative, bubbly, polite and clumsy writer. I love to write it claims me down. I grew up in Minnesota in St. Michael and I love to write outside. My book ideas are unique and creative and each of the characters represents me a little I put a little of me in each of the characters and they deal with problems of today but I put my heart and soul into these books and I hope you enjoy them. Love you all! ♥